A House by the Sea

Joanne Ryder pictures by Melissa Sweet

Morrow Junior Books
New York

For Larry, my seaside buddy, with love
—J. R.

To my nephew, Dylan, with love
—M. S.

Watercolors were used for the full-color artwork. The text type is 16–point Schneidler medium.

Text copyright © 1994 by Joanne Ryder
Illustrations copyright © 1994 by Melissa Sweet

All rights reserved. No part of this book may be reproduced or utilized in any form or by any means,
electronic or mechanical, including photocopying, recording, or by any information storage and retrieval system,
without permission in writing from the Publisher. Inquiries should be addressed to
William Morrow and Company, Inc., 1350 Avenue of the Americas, New York, NY 10019.
Printed in Hong Kong by South China Printing Company (1988) Ltd.
1 2 3 4 5 6 7 8 9 10

Library of Congress Cataloging-in-Publication Data
A house by the sea / Joanne Ryder ; pictures by Melissa Sweet.
p.   cm.   Summary: Describes what it would be like to live in a little house by the sea
and frolic with seals and crabs and other sea creatures.
ISBN 0-688-12675-8 (trade). — ISBN 0-688-12676-6 (library)   [1. Seashore—Fiction.   2. Marine animals—Fiction.
3. Stories in rhyme.]   I. Sweet, Melissa, ill.   II. Title.   PZ8.3.R9595Ho   1994   [E]—dc20   93-22149   CIP   AC

If I could live in a little house,
I'd live in a house by the sea.

Some days I'd visit the frisky seals,
and some days they'd visit me.

FISH-EYED
PIE

We'd walk in the rain,
those seals and I,
till we'd stop for a slice
of fish-eyed pie.

When I got too wet
or they got too dry,
we'd hug and we'd run
and we'd yell, "Good-bye."

I'd watch and I'd wave
to those seals in the sea,
and their flippers would splash,
waving back at me.

If I could live in a little house,
I'd live in a house by the sea.

And I'd whisper at night
when the moon was bright,
"Would you please give a wish to me?"

And I'd wish I could fly
in the star-speckled sky
and wash my face in a cloud,

and I'd sing to the moon
a silly sea tune till he
laughed and laughed out loud.

Then I'd land on a whale
with a black-and-white tail
who would rock me fast asleep,

and she'd carry me home
on a crest of foam
over the waters deep.

If I could live in a little house,
I'd live in a house by the sea.

An octopus would live next door
and take good care of me.

With an arm doing this,
and an arm doing that,
he'd cook and make my bed.

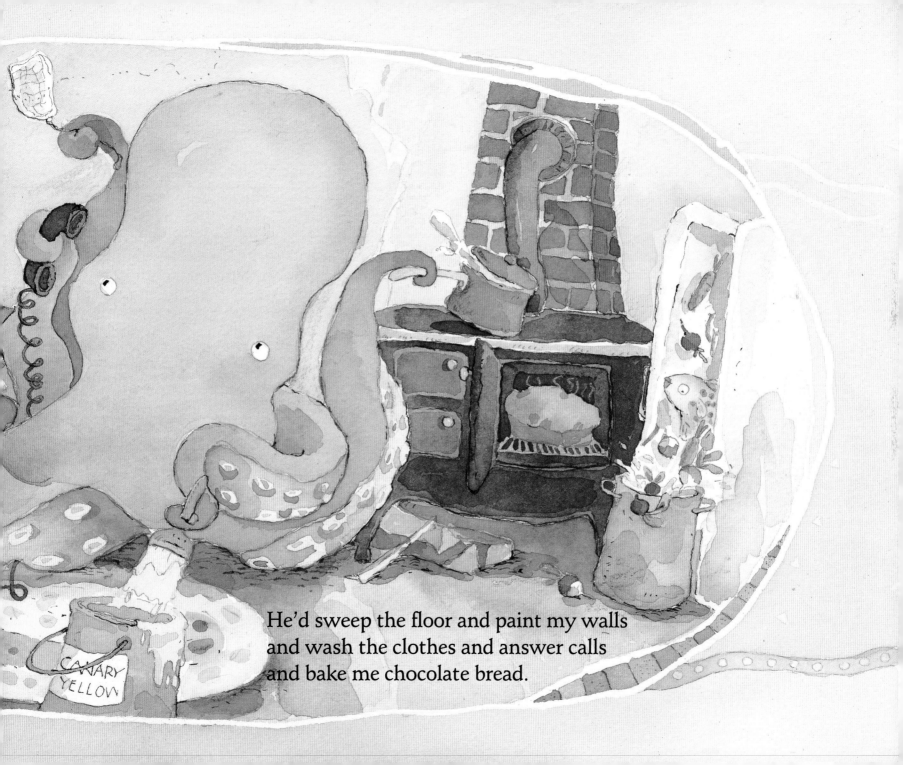

He'd sweep the floor and paint my walls
and wash the clothes and answer calls
and bake me chocolate bread.

I'd read him stories
while he worked
and serve him seaweed tea,

and I would thank him very much
for taking care of me.

If I could live in a little house,
I'd live in a house by the sea.
Some days I'd catch the sea in a pail.
Some days the sea would catch me!

I'd be wet, wet, wet
from my nose to my toes,
bobbing away from the shore

till the sea changed its mind
and carried me back
and tossed me alongside my door.

When I can live in a little house,
I'll live in a house by the sea.

And I'll play in the sand,
dancing hand in hand
with a crab who is fond of me.

We'll play crab games
and trade our names,
so if you come calling me,

she'll hold out a claw
to shake your paw
as friendly as she can be.

HOUSE BY THE SEA

CRAB BY THE BAY

Just ask the way
to the *crab* by the bay
and she'll point
the path to *me*.

Whenever you come
to the little house
that sits at the edge of the sea,

if you like, we can play
in the sand all day
a crab game, or two, or three.

And I'll call you, *Me,*
and you'll call me, *You,*

and no one will know
who is who
but us two
as we dance
round the rim
of the sea.